John Walker Pattison was born in the wonderful seaside town of South Shields 64 years ago.

He is a long-suffering but dedicated Newcastle United supporter; however, there is little doubt that the crucial hinge in John's life is his beautiful wife, June, and his family. "Nothing is more important than family," says John.

He recently retired from his post as a senior clinical nurse specialist in haematology at his local hospital, a place that established his cancer diagnosis in 1975; he is humbled to be one of the longest living cancer survivors in the UK at 46 years post diagnosis.

His interests include Native American photography and exploring parts of America unseen by tourists.

Strange Trips and Weird Adventures

John Walker Pattison

AUSTIN MACAULEY PUBLISHERS™

LONDON • CAMBRIDGE • NEW YORK • SHARJAH

A CIP catalogue record for this title is available from the British Library.

ISBN 9781398416581 (Paperback)
ISBN 9781398416598 (ePub e-book)

www.austinmacauley.com

First Published (2021)
Austin Macauley Publishers Ltd
25 Canada Square
Canary Wharf
London
E14 5LQ

To Daniel, my bestest ever buddy.

A special thank you to my sister-in-law, Diane Ward, for all her help and support, especially with my grammar.

My wonderful wife, June, for the unswerving support.

To children everywhere; let your dreams take you wherever you want to go.

Introduction

Daniel, the inquisitive young rascal with little fear and a devilish sense of humour, cuddled next to his best friend, Grandpa, whom he warmly called Papa. Outside, the snow was cascading from the heavens during what was a bitterly cold winter's evening. Daniel safely sat next to Papa; the log fire roared a fiery glow of warmness. A twelve-year-old with a tussle of untidy but beautiful dark hair, his piercing blue eyes could melt the largest of large icebergs while they had already melted a thousand and one hearts, his innocent smile hid a spoonful of mischief, especially when he was with Papa. In turn, despite Papa being sixty-four years young, he was always on the look-out for his next challenge. His thin face was complemented by a pair of multi-coloured glasses. He had short black hair and a goatee that was speckled with grey, a long nose and a love for Daniel that knew no limits.

Daniel tilted his head towards Papa, smiled an impish smile and asked, "Tell me about one of your weird adventures."

Laughing, Papa simply gazed at the boy. Daniel knew that look; something was going on in that mind of his.

No one could tell a tale like Papa, not even Pinocchio. What he had done, where he had been was unbelievable; so unbelievable that some said, particularly Grandma, he could sell ice to the Eskimos and in response Papa would say, "Actually, I already have!"

Yes, Papa had done it all; he claimed to have discovered Captain Broderick McCaffery's treasure beyond the Enchanted Forest and on another weird adventure he had found his way into the Marmalade Kingdom making friends with Finbar Floptrop, the friendliest fox in the kingdom. Daniel would listen intently to those tales. Papa confessed that he had climbed Mount Everest barefoot and had slurped tea with the Queen of England. Papa told Daniel of his fights with lions, tigers and even a great white shark. He had captained England to win the World Cup and had won the Monaco Grand Prix in a car that he built from junk, found in the backyard; but Daniel's most favourite tale was when Papa explained how he played keyboards in the greatest rock band ever, "Wind of Change" and had headlined at Stinky Farty Park Festival. But Papa's greatest claim, however, was that he had rid Splodge City of the most fearsome gunslingers in "The Wild West", Wild Will Hickory Dickory Jock.

What Papa hadn't done, well, quite frankly, it wasn't worth doing, or so he said. A fighter pilot, an undercover secret agent and he had even captured the Loch Ness monster before letting it go again. Stories that Daniel accepted with a pinch of salt, still he loved Papa with all his heart.

So, as the log fire crackled and the flames flickered this way and that way, throwing out its comforting heat, Papa sat deep in thought, thinking to himself, and the think that he was thinking was, *It's about time for another weird adventure but how do we manage that and stay out of trouble with Grandma?*

On most days, he and Daniel could easily find trouble without even trying; right now, however, Papa was aiming not just to stay out of trouble, but also to avoid annoying Grandma as she was still mad about the

terrible trouble he had gotten into last time he returned from a weird adventure.

It was just then that Papa looked at Daniel and said, "Did I ever tell you about the time I went to the Moon?"

Daniel gave Papa one of his looks and shook his head in disbelief. "And why did you go to the Moon, Papa?" Daniel asked.

"Grandma needed some special cheese," he replied, and a smile stretched across his face. "Cheese that is only available on the Moon. You do know that the Moon is made of cheese, don't you?"

"No, Papa, I thought that was just a story!"

"Well," continued Papa, "instead of telling you all about the Moon, why don't I take you there and you can see for yourself? As a surprise, we can bring some cheese back for Grandma."

"Do you think that will get you back into her good books, Papa?" Daniel asked, before laughing.

"Well, perhaps only for a short while or until the next strange trip," Papa added.

Daniel thought for a moment, and then rubbed his nose before asking, "So just how would we get there?"

"Easy," replied Papa. "We'll build a Moon rocket of course; it shouldn't take us long and we'll be back before tea."

Chapter One

So the next morning, out into the backyard, the two eager adventurers went to collect what they needed to build a Moon rocket. They started by clearing the snow that had been neatly deposited overnight. Papa gathered some wood, some odd pieces of metal, an old washing machine motor, a broken broom handle, a length of rubber hose, a very large tube of plastic and smaller lumps of plastic in different shapes and, not forgetting one of Daniel's old toy boxes.

"One thing we mustn't forget, Daniel."

"What?" asked the boy intrigued by the whole adventure.

"Come with me, my young astronaut," said Papa taking the boy back into the kitchen. "If Grandma doesn't have any of what I'm looking for, then the trip will be cancelled," declared Papa.

Daniel thought to himself, *This was a poor excuse for Papa to say the trip is off.*

Papa rummaged through the kitchen draws until after most of the contents had been scattered all over the floor, creating one heck of a mess.

Daniel thought, *Grandma certainly wouldn't like that; Papa has obviously forgotten that he was trying to stay out of trouble.*

Papa shouted, "This is what we need!"

Holding a large roll of tin foil above his head in triumph, he told Daniel, "The foil must cover the rocket from top to bottom for safety reasons."

"Oh," Daniel replied and tried his best not to laugh. "I

thought we'd be cooking on the way, Papa!"

Ignoring Daniel's sarcasm, Papa looked very thoughtful, then said, "That's not a bad idea, it's a long way and we might get a bit hungry, let's see what Grandma has in the fridge."

So as the search continued for this, that and the other, the two boys went back outside.

Papa called to Daniel, "Can you search for a length of washing line and one red brick please; we can't go to the Moon without them."

Daniel found the items and called to Papa, "I'm so cold, and my fingers are so numb, I think they might fall off!"

Papa looked at the boy and replied, "This is not cold, I remember the time I climbed Mount Everest barefoot. Now that was cold!" Papa just could not help himself.

Daniel shook his head and said, "I'm going inside to get warm."

"OK," said Papa. "See if you can find some buttons for the rocket!"

Daniel went inside and knew exactly where to look; Grandma's knitting basket.

Outside, Papa finally found what he was searching for among what now had become mucky, dirty snow; a pot of red paint, a pot of blue paint and the rusting wing from an old car.

"Ah," said Papa to himself. "This will be perfect for the rocket's nose cone."

Just then, Daniel opened the back door, his breath visible in the cold air as he called to Papa, "Do we have everything yet?"

Papa looked at Daniel and scratched his head.

"Let me think," said Papa. "Anything else we might need? Ah yes!" he exclaimed; Papa often talked to himself when he was planning. "Sherbet, a very large bag of sherbet!"

"But why?" asked the boy.

"Sherbet is essential for the engine. Without it, we won't get far. I'm sure Grandma had some in her baking drawer."

Thinking of what might be in Grandma's fridge, Daniel then asked, "Can we take some chocolate for the journey, Papa?"

Seldom, if ever, would Papa decline any request from his grandson and replied, "Definitely!" Continuing, "If we start to build the rocket now, we can set off for the Moon tomorrow morning in order to get back home again before bedtime."

And so, the two best friends set off building the Moon rocket, singing football songs as they did so. First into place was the large plastic tube, big enough for both of them to fit into. The piece of the old car was placed neatly on top and Papa took his home-made glue made from flour, water, black treacle, a teaspoon of cough medicine and a secret ingredient that only Papa knew and spread it evenly around the outside edges. He then gave the sticky substance to Daniel who climbed inside and smeared the glue all around the nose cone. Before the glue was dry, the two boys covered the outer body of the rocket with the tin foil, carefully cutting around the window and then painted it red and blue. Papa then gave Daniel the job of attaching the washing machine motor to the rubber hose at one end and to his old toy box at the other. "Once you've done that, glue them down so that they are safe for take-off and landing."

The remaining parts of the lunar rocket were put in place and, just as Papa had said, the rocket was complete by the time Grandma had returned from the shops.

"And what have my two boys been up to?" she felt compelled to ask, knowing fine well that they must have been up to something, after all, Papa was always up to something, usually mischief.

Daniel was the first to reply, hugging Grandma as he said, "We built a cool Moon rocket from the junk in the backyard."

Grandma just smiled and said, "Well, that sounds harmless. I'll make some tea then, anyone have any suggestions?"

"Scrambled egg, salmon and huckleberry jam, please," Daniel declared without hesitation, as that was his favourite, although he would eat anything with huckleberry jam on it.

After tea the three sat 'round the log fire enjoying its warmth; Daniel talked about the impending weird adventure to the Moon, wondering whether he would meet 'the man in the Moon'. Grandma sipped her cup of tea and Papa slurped his whisky, suggesting that as they had a long day ahead, Daniel should head off to bed, quickly adding, "Astronauts do need their sleep."

Daniel jumped up, hugged Papa and then kissed Grandma and without question made his way to bed.

The next morning, Papa and Daniel got dressed, finished

breakfast and headed out into the backyard where the rocket stood proudly waiting for them.

"It's a splendid rocket," said Papa with pride.

"It sure is, Papa," replied Daniel, adding, "let's climb in."

Papa climbed up into the rocket, closely followed by Daniel. Papa asked Daniel to pour just enough sherbet into the toy box; it went through a special funnel and into the engine.

"Are we ready to go, Papa?" Daniel excitedly asked.

"Yes," he replied. "Can you start the countdown please, Daniel?"

Daniel eagerly and yet calmly started the countdown as if he had been trained by NASA. "10, 9, 8..."

Papa pushed forward the first lever which was made from the broken broom handle and two green lights flashed.

Daniel thought, *They look just like Grandma's favourite garden lanterns.* "7, 6, 5..."

Papa pushed a large silver button and Daniel was sure that was a button that had fallen off Grandma's cardigan on the washing line – *Oh dear, more trouble!*

Just then, a robotic voice said, "Fasten seat belts and get ready for take-off."

Daniel looked around, curious as to where the robotic voice was coming from, only to find Papa with a hollow tube pressed to his mouth and repeating the words, "Fasten your seat belts."

The boy smirked, and then continued, "4, 3, 2 and 1."

The rocket shook as if they were in the middle of a hurricane; Daniel thought that at any minute it would all collapse around them but Papa had built many rockets so he was confident that the space ship would launch safely. "Hold tight, Daniel!" shouted Papa, and just as the rocket shook, there was an ear-splitting explosion spilling smoke into the backyard before the sound of a terrifying SHRIEK! A startled black and white cat appeared from the smoke, its hair standing on end, its whiskers singed to a frazzle, an angry look on its face. It leapt over the wall and ran down the lane. With a splutter and a clatter, the rocket lifted smoothly from the ground, rising swiftly into the air. The two would-be astronauts waved frantically, unaware whether Grandma could see them or not. Below them they could see the children playing in the lane and who were getting smaller and smaller until eventually they were just specks on the ground.

Leaving Earth further and further behind, they sailed through the marshmallow clouds and out of the other side to discover radiant blue skies. The rocket was performing ever so well as it weaved its way through the largest rainbow anyone had ever seen. As the Earth was getting smaller and smaller, Daniel could now see the Moon looming as they spiralled through the blackness of space. Strapped into their seats, Papa and Daniel gazed out of the window as the rocket travelled into the darkness of outer space and on through a million twinkling stars to approach the Moon just before lunch, exactly as Papa had planned. The rocket juddered, shook three times and created a blast of smoke before Papa reversed it onto the surface of the Moon as if he had done all of this before.

"A perfect landing, Papa," said Daniel.

Papa grabbed the single red brick, took the length of washing line, tied it not once but twice around the brick, opened the rocket door and dropped it onto the Moon's surface. "That will keep the rocket safe until we are ready to leave," closing the door afterwards.

"Well, I'm a bit hungry now," Papa said. "Let's see what we have to eat before we go and explore. Maybe we can start with a bit of chocolate, Daniel?"

A momentary pause and Daniel whispered a response, "Oh, Papa, I ate the chocolate as we passed through the stars."

Papa secretly knew the chocolate had been scoffed earlier in the flight and smiled to himself.

"Lucky then that I brought some crisps and huckleberry jam sandwiches," declared Papa.

"Any for me?" Daniel asked tentatively.

"Of course," said Papa, and the two tucked into their snacks and a cup of orange juice.

Daniel was ready and raring to leave the rocket ship and for the much-awaited Moon walk.

"The air is very thin up here," said Papa, "so you must wear this." Papa handed Daniel a special space helmet made from cardboard and cellotape, with a plastic visor so that Daniel could see everything that was happening on the Moon. It had been painted a bright orange colour just so Papa could see Daniel at all times while they were exploring the lunar surface.

Daniel was excited about leaving the rocket so he carefully placed the Moon helmet on his head and as he stepped out of the rocket onto the surface of the Moon, he declared, "It's cheese, Papa!"

Papa laughed before saying, "Yes, I did tell you that."

Stepping onto the surface of the Moon was fun, Daniel and Papa bounced up and floated down, bounced forward and floated down again as if they were on a bed of balloons.

Daniel twisted his face, asking, "What's that terrible smell?" Papa laughed again at the boy. "It's cheese. More cheese than you could wish for in a life-time."

Daniel then plucked a large chunk of stringy cheese from the surface of the Moon, pushed it underneath his space helmet and munched away. He loved the cheese and said to Papa, "It tastes wonderful, just a shame we don't have any huckleberry jam."

The two explorers bounced across the Moon's surface, laughing and chasing one another, climbing up the Moon hills and then rolling back down. After running across the Moon's surface for what seemed like miles, Daniel sat down to rest, forgetting about Papa for just a moment.

Minutes later, he heard a distant voice echo his name; "Daniel?" came the distorted sound. The boy looked for Papa but he was nowhere to be seen; now he was worried! He looked all around where they had chased one another only minutes earlier but he could see nothing of his beloved Papa, only his footprints in the Moon dust where they had played, then again, the eerie sound "Daniel", it seemed to echo across the surface of the Moon. Accepting that he was now just a tiny bit afraid, he slowly walked towards the sound. "Daniel?" There it was again! All kinds of thoughts filled his head; perhaps it was a scary alien or even the 'man in the Moon' but, most importantly, where was Papa? He had walked only a few more steps when he saw Papa's head appearing out of a large hole. Daniel grabbed Papa's arm and pulled and pulled until the old man popped out of the hole.

"Daniel, thank heavens! I thought I would never get out of here," said Papa.

"Gosh, what happened?" asked Daniel.

"Well, Daniel, I don't know if you've noticed but the Moon is made of lots of different cheese, so some parts are crumbly and others are riddled with holes. Unfortunately, just as you sat down to rest, I fell into a large hole and I had to go through a lot of tunnels to try and find my way out, that's when I became stuck in that cheese hole; thank goodness you heard me calling out!"

Daniel giggled a nervous giggle, relieved that Papa was safe but still tickled at how Papa had fallen into a cheese hole. They headed back to the rocket ship; Papa was still a bit shaken about his experience in the cheese holes when they came across something they didn't expect. Daniel was first to see it and called to Papa.

"Look what I've found, a flag."

Indeed he had, a flag of 15 stripes and lots of stars. The flag was clearly very old and the colour had faded. With a huge puff from Papa, most of the dust cleared, causing both Daniel and Papa to sneeze uncontrollably.

Once the sneezing had stopped, Daniel looked around nervously and said, "Someone else must be here?"

"No," said Papa, explaining that this flag was from 1969 when a man named Armstrong from America had put it there. Daniel was never one to question how Papa knew this as he did know lots of stuff. Papa explained that Neil Armstrong and Buzz Aldrin had landed in their craft called The Eagle back when Papa was only twelve years old.

"Did they come looking for cheese, Papa?" asked Daniel.

"They did," replied Papa. "At that time there was a plague of mice in America and they ate all the cheese so there was a competition to see who could find enough cheese to feed everyone.

"Neil and Buzz had heard that the Moon was made of cheese so that was an obvious place to look, and they were right as they won the competition!"

"But how did they get all that cheese home?" asked Daniel.

"Well, that's a funny story," Papa said. "Their rocket was much bigger than ours and they had a very large parachute to help them land safely, but the parachute was so big, it took up lots of space in the rocket. So the astronauts, Neil and Buzz, decided to get rid of the parachute to make room for the cheese."

"That was a good idea," said Daniel, "but how did they land safely without a parachute?"

"Well, those astronauts were very clever," Papa explained. "They loaded all the cheese on board and during their journey home, they melted all the cheese down into stringy cheese and knitted a trio of parachutes, which they attached to the rocket through a special door at the back of the ship. Of course, the rocket was much lighter without all the cheese on board and they safely splashed down in the North Pacific Ocean."

"That was clever," said Daniel. "But how did the people get the cheese if it was made into three parachutes?" asked Daniel.

"Oh, that was simple," replied Papa. "After the astronauts landed, they collected up the parachute, melted the cheese again and made it into small portions so they could distribute it to all the people."

"Wow, Papa, just wow!"

"This is the best weird adventure," declared Daniel, as he and Papa headed back to their rocket ship. Daniel had taken lots of photographs to show his mum and dad on his return to Earth; after all, he had to prove he'd been to the Moon. But the last thing they had to do before leaving the Moon was to collect some cheese for Grandma. Daniel crawled about on his hands and knees pulling chunks of different-coloured cheese to put into the bag they had brought with them especially for the cheese. Every now and then, he would place a handful of the cheese into his mouth until eventually, he turned to Papa, rubbed his tummy and said, "No more cheese for me."

So once they had filled the bag with enough cheese to feed an army, they climbed back into the space rocket, closing the door behind them. "Can we come back to the Moon on another day, Papa?"

"Of course we can, but we still have other strange trips and weird adventures to do," said Papa. "But for now, let's get ready to head home and prepare for take-off. Start your countdown, Astronaut Daniel," instructed Papa.

"10, 9, 8..." but when Papa flicked the switch, nothing happened.

"Oh dear," said Papa, trying to remain calm.

"What's happened, Papa?" Daniel nervously asked.

"Push that orange button please, Daniel."

Daniel pushed the button as instructed and a robotic voice said, "Rocket cannot lift off, still tied down."

"Aha!" declared Papa with a huge sigh of relief. Papa once again opened the rocket door, climbed down to the surface of the Moon and untied the length of washing line attached to the red brick which had held the rocket on the surface of the Moon.

Back into the rocket, Papa instructed Daniel to once again start the countdown.

"10, 9, 8..." Papa flicked the switch and as the sherbet

entered the engine, the rocket started to gently shake, preparing to take off. "7, 6, 5..."

"Are we ready for lift off, Daniel?"

"Yes, Papa," responded the boy. "4, 3, 2, 1..." and lift off they did; up, up and away they went leaving the Moon surface behind.

As the Moon got smaller and smaller, Daniel gazed at the twinkling stars dancing against the background of absolute darkness. Another rocket passed them by and Daniel waved frantically at the craft but was unable to tell if anyone was returning his wave.

Only minutes later, a shooting star whizzed alongside as Papa shouted, "Make a wish, Daniel."

He thought to himself, closed his eyes tightly and wished a wish like never before. He then opened his eyes and then said, "Wow, Papa, just wow!"

Leaving the darkness of space behind them, down they went, into the clouds and slowing down as they drew nearer to Earth, landing in the backyard just before tea time, exactly as Papa had planned.

Before they opened the rocket door, ready to climb out, Papa asked Daniel, "How was that then for a weird adventure?"

Daniel replied in four words, "Wow, Papa, just wow!"

This made Papa smile.

Just as the boys got out of the Moon rocket, Grandma opened the back door and greeted them with a cough and a splutter as she breathed in the dust caused by the landing rocket.

Daniel immediately shouted, "Grandma, Grandma, we've been to the Moon."

"You must be exhausted," she replied.

"Yes, I'm ready for tea but I couldn't eat any more cheese!"

"Well, that sounds exciting, but I've had a very strange day," Grandma said. "I was going to make some sherbet cakes for tea but I couldn't find the sherbet, so I thought I would do some more washing instead, but couldn't find the spare washing line! I'd also hoped we could sit in the front room after tea with a few snacks and you could tell me all about your adventure – but I couldn't find the chocolate or the crisps. I suppose it's a bit cold now, and it will be dark soon, and my cardigan has a button missing and I can't find my green lanterns! It's all very weird, I don't suppose either of you know anything about that?" asked Grandma.

Daniel and Papa just looked at each other and Daniel smiled his most innocent smile before declaring, "No, Grandma, as you know we've been out all day, but don't worry, we'll just have something else for tea and we'll be very happy sitting in front of the television and we'll tell you all about our journey to the Moon."

After tea, Daniel found his favourite spot, wedged between Grandma and Papa, but before he could relive his lunar experience, Daniel fell sound asleep, his pockets stuffed with cheese and a beaming smile still etched on his face.

Chapter Two

The following weekend when Daniel went to stay with Grandma and Papa, as he did every weekend, he was greeted with lots of hugs from his grandparents and in return, he delivered his infectious smile.

"Let's read about grey-blue humpback whales, Papa."

This was without doubt Daniel's favourite subject.

Papa looked at Daniel and said, "Did I ever tell you about the time I swam with the grey-blue humpback whales?"

Remembering their recent trip to the Moon, Daniel wasn't surprised to hear Papa had more weird adventures up his sleeve so he just said, "Tell me more, Papa," as he snuggled up with his best friend.

"Better still," continued Papa, "why don't I take you to see the grey-blue humpback whales?"

Intrigued, Daniel quickly responded, "Definitely, when can we go and how will we get there?"

"Well," responded Papa, "if we build a submarine this afternoon, perhaps we can set sail tomorrow. What do you think, Grandma?"

Grandma smiled and nodded her agreement to the plan, adding, "I'll stay at home, because when you boys return, you'll both be ready for dinner, but don't get into any trouble!"

Papa turned to Grandma and said, "There are lots of dangers in the oceans, but we'll be alright. It's not the first time I've sailed to the hidden depths, you know."

Daniel and Papa set off to find what they needed to build a special submarine. An old canoe that had lain in the corner of the yard for so long would be very useful. Two bubble making machines that Papa used when he played in the band 'Wind of Change' would make perfect propellers, one on either side of the submarine. They decided to use some of the parts from the successful Moon rocket that still stood proudly at the top of the yard; importantly, the engine could now be used to power the underwater vessel. Papa found ten unused birthday balloons that would be ideal to help the submarine float. They also found some string, some of Papa's very special glue and tape, while Daniel shouted, "Papa, don't forget the sherbet for the engine."

"Well remembered, Daniel," said Papa. "Let's hope Grandma bought some more after our Moon trip!"

Just as the inseparable duo finished searching for important components, Papa remembered an old steering wheel from an unused video gaming machine which would help steer the submarine.

Just then, a voice called, "You boys can finish building that thing after dinner." Grandma beckoned the two in for something to eat.

Papa and Daniel washed their hands and sat down to dinner that had been so lovingly prepared by Grandma for her two favourite boys. Daniel suggested that the submarine should have a name and the two agreed that it should be called *HMS Humpback Whale.*

As they finished eating, Daniel asked, "Can we take some chocolate on our journey, Papa, and I promise not to eat it *all* myself."

"Ha ha, of course, Daniel," he said. Thinking, *That'll be more trouble from Grandma when she discovers the missing chocolate.*

So, they set about building the submarine with the parts they had collected; *This bit goes here and that bit goes there;* they had three used toy containers that could be used as the top part of the submarine.

"These," Papa held up two bubble machines, "are ideal for our thrusters and will help direct the vessel," he said, before adding, "Oh yes, have you still got that packet of bubble gum, Daniel?"

"Yes, Papa," the boy replied.

"Then make sure you put it in your pocket when we leave." Daniel was perplexed, but trusted Papa like no other and didn't question the need to take bubble gum.

Time ticked by and before they knew anymore, it was getting dark as the final components of the submarine were assembled. Daniel grabbed what was left of the pot of red paint and started to decorate the submarine.

"Well," said Papa. "I think we can be proud of this, Daniel." They embraced each other in celebration of their victorious build.

"Tomorrow, we'll load *HMS Humpback Whale* onto the car and set sail from the long beach," which was only five minutes' drive from Papa's house.

Into Papa's house they triumphantly marched just as Grandma was taking a pasta bake out of the oven. Hungry from their exertions, the two boys devoured the pasta bake and then sat together as Daniel asked, "What will it be like under the sea, Papa?"

Tilting his head to look at Daniel, Papa spoke quietly, "There are many dangers down there. First of all..." he began.

Daniel was now engrossed if not just a little afraid and seeing this fear, Grandma interrupted Papa and said, "Don't frighten the lad with those weird tales. Anyhow, I think it's time for bed."

Daniel kissed Grandma, hugged Papa and without a question headed off to bed.

The next morning, the sun had risen, leaving a glorious orange tinge to the sky.

A great day to launch a submarine, thought Papa.

After a good breakfast of pancakes and huckleberry jam, Papa and Daniel loaded *HMS Humpback Whale* onto the trailer, ready for its transport to the sea.

Once all secured, Grandma drove the two deep sea adventurers to the long beach where they unloaded the submarine and prepared for its launch. Papa asked Daniel to fill the engine with sherbet and as the waves lapped around the vessel, the two boys excitedly climbed aboard, ready to be swept out to sea and commence their search for the grey-blue humpback whale. Just before closing the lid, Daniel and Papa waved an affectionate wave to Grandma.

It wasn't long before the tide had engulfed the submarine and dragged the craft far out to sea.

"Start the engine," Papa instructed Daniel. *Vroom, swoosh, chug, chug, chug* and off they went diving deeper and deeper into the realms of the great unknown. There were three windows in the submarine; one on the top of the vessel so they could see where they were going and, more importantly, so that they avoided bumping into any fish or even a whale, and one either side, one for Daniel and one for Papa.

Daniel was speechless, which was most unusual, but also amazed at how clear the water was. He smiled at the multi-coloured fish, and waved at a grey seal that flicked a waving flipper as it swam past. As the submarine neared the bottom of the sea, hovering just above the sea bed, an army of crabs and a family of shrimps scurried behind the seaweed-covered rocks. Daniel laughed at such frantic activity, and as the crabs and shrimps disappeared from view, a huge cod fish peered through Daniel's window, much to his entertainment. The cod fish appeared to be talking to Daniel, but sadly, Daniel could not hear what the fish was saying. He could, however, see dozens and dozens of bubbles coming from its mouth; it appeared to be chatting to Daniel. The young boy signalled his friendship with his thumb to the fish, and waved with his other hand.

As the two intrepid sailors happily cruised along, they passed an old wreck lying sideways on the bottom of the sea.

"Keep your eyes open, Daniel!"

The boy detected nervousness in Papa's voice and asked, "What am I looking for, Papa?"

Papa was silent before explaining, "That is the wreck of Captain Broderick McCaffery and strange things happen from time to time."

"Like what?" Daniel asked with some concern.

"Oh, just weird things," Papa replied, clearly not wanting to explain any more than that.

Papa breathed a huge sigh of relief as they passed the wreck without incident, and as they did so, Daniel spotted a huge conger eel lying among a forest of seaweed, swaying back and forth as if dancing together with the tide. It looked up at the submarine and without giving them a second thought continued to practice its own dance moves. Shoals of silvery fish paraded ahead of a large sunfish that appeared to be searching for someone or something.

Then, Papa called out from his position behind the steering wheel, "Let's make our way to see those grey-blue humpback whales."

"Yeah!" called Daniel.

"OK, Daniel, set our course for 45 degrees please, and I'll inflate ten balloons to help the submarine rise from the bottom of the sea."

Within minutes, the submarine started to rise and soon broke the surface and the moment it did, there was the incredible sight of not one, not two but three grey-blue humpback whales frolicking in the crystal blue waters only metres from the submarine. One by one, they would take turns leaping from the water to create the biggest and best splash Daniel had ever seen. Waves that made the submarine bob up and down like a cork in water.

The acrobatic display of the whales only lasted a few minutes before the largest of the creatures spotted the submarine and swam gently towards it, pressing its large eye against the front window; Daniel wasn't at all afraid, calling and waving to the giant mammal and in return, the whale winked and smiled at Daniel before returning to the other two. It was then that the smallest of the whales came up to Daniel's window and pushed against the submarine, shoving it in a sideward direction, moving it faster than it had ever travelled. Once again, the whale gave a wink, a smile and a shrill cry towards Daniel, and before the two sub-mariners knew anything else, all three whales were gone.

"Wow, Papa, just wow!" exclaimed Daniel. "Those whales were so friendly; do you think we'll ever see them again?"

"Well, you never know!" Papa replied.

After so much excitement, Papa suggested it was now time for the chocolate.

Daniel gave Papa that apologetic look, "Sorry, Papa, I ate the chocolate when we saw the crabs earlier."

"Never mind, Daniel, luckily I brought some crisps and orange juice."

Munching on the crisps and sipping his orange juice, Daniel had a permanent glow on his face, a reflection of his satisfaction after seeing the whales.

"About time we headed home, I think," said Papa. So they turned the submarine around, let all the air out of the ten balloons and took the *HMS Humpback Whale* under the water to make their way back to the long beach where Grandma would be patiently waiting.

Papa tugged at the controls and smoothly turned the submarine around before calling to Daniel, "Full steam ahead."

They had only sailed for a few moments when the submarine suddenly jolted to a halt. Daniel looked out of his window and shouted, "I think we are tangled in some seaweed, Papa."

The submarine made an eerie creaking sound as water started to *GUSH* into the front. "That's not seaweed, Daniel!"

Papa frantically called out, "That's Squidly Ridley, a giant squid that lives in the wreck of Captain Broderick McCaffery."

The Squid had wrapped its silver and gold tentacles all around the submarine and was refusing to release its deathly stranglehold, its jet-black eyes the size of dinner plates peered through the vessel's window.

"What do we do, Papa?" Daniel asked as a solitary tear rolled down his cheek.

"Have you got that bubble gum?"

Daniel fumbled through his pockets and pulled out a packet of bubble gum, showing it to Papa.

"Right," said Papa, trying his very best not to show Daniel how scared he was, "put it in your mouth and chew as quickly as you can!"

As Daniel started to chew and chew, his jaw began to ache. He could see Papa rummaging about in search of something, but what?

"Got it!" called Papa and he held high what remained of the packet of sherbet. Dashing forward, Papa took the packet of sherbet and squeezed it through the damaged part of the submarine. Papa struggled as water was still rushing into their vessel but, as soon as Squidly Ridley saw the packet emerge from the broken submarine, he seized it and in one fell swoop engulfed it. Only seconds passed, Daniel still chewing as if his life depended upon it, the submarine rolled, still in the deathly grip of the giant squid, then...

Ah, ah, ah atishoooooooo!

The sherbet that Squidly Ridley had greedily devoured irritated the squid so much that he sneezed a sneeze so big, he released his hold on the submarine and rocketed back towards the wreck and wedged himself between the ship's timbers.

Papa then called to Daniel, "Quick, spit that bubble gum into my hand!"

Daniel, relieved to be able to stop chewing, deposited the gum into Papa's shaking hand. Papa took the pink bubble gum and plugged the hole. Instantly, the water stopped entering their vessel.

"That was a close call," Papa said with relief.

Daniel smiled a scared smile at his bestest buddy and said, "Wow, Papa, just wow!"

"Right!" said Papa. "Let's head home, that's enough excitement for one day."

The vessel now sailed effortlessly through the waters, zigging and zagging to avoid the misshapen rocks along their route. Two haddock swam in front of the submarine for a long while as if magically showing them the way. The water was getting shallower and shallower, meaning they were about to reach the beach. As the tide took control of the craft, the submarine slid onto the soft sand of the long beach, safely back home.

Papa and Daniel clambered out of the submarine. A warm smile from Grandma greeted them.

She asked, "Did you see the whales?"

"Yeah, Grandma, not one, not two but three and they were so cool."

"You can tell me all about it over dinner; I've made mince pie and roast potatoes."

Daniel smiled, gave Grandma a huge hug and said, "Sounds good, I'm so hungry," turning and gesturing to Papa to hurry up.

"Well, I also thought a chocolate pudding for a sweet would be nice but I couldn't find the chocolate. I don't suppose you two know anything about that?" said Grandma suspiciously.

Papa and Daniel looked at each other and Daniel, with his sweetest smile, said, "No, Grandma, as you know we've been out all afternoon."

Naturally, they never told Grandma about the encounter with the giant squid as that would have gotten Papa into more trouble than ever before.

Chapter Three

For Daniel, the next week seemed to drag ever so slowly as the young boy was so keen to get back to Grandma and Papa's house and continue his strange trips. He'd go to bed each night wondering what the next weird adventure could be.

The time eventually ticked by, and early on Saturday morning, Daniel was excited like never before. He knew that today was the day he was headed back to see his grandparents; his mind was racing with thoughts of what Papa would have planned.

The boy was dressed, teeth brushed and away down the stairs hoping that his breakfast was ready and waiting for him, as it usually was.

"Going somewhere, Daniel?" asked his mum with a wry smile.

Daniel laughed, "It's Saturday, and you know that's my day for Grandma and Papa."

Less than an hour later, Papa and Grandma arrived and were greeted with smiles and the biggest hug a boy could deliver to the people he loved.

"What are we going to do today, Papa?" asked the keen young mind.

"Oh, let's just wait and see," suggested Papa, knowing that his words would simply intrigue Daniel all the more. "Now," said Papa, "big hugs for Mum and Dad and we'll get going."

At Papa's house, the two boys sat in the den discussing both the trip to the Moon and the visit to see the grey-blue humpback whales.

"So what is our next adventure, Papa?"

"All in good time, Daniel, all in good time."

Later in the evening, as Papa was preparing to light the log burner, Daniel shivered.

"Hurry up and light that fire, Papa, I'm really cold!" he said.

As the fire came to life, the flames giving a warm glow, Papa said, "If you think this is cold, let me tell you about the time I went to the Arctic Circle."

"Do tell me more," Daniel requested.

Papa smiled and simply said, "Instead of telling you about it, why don't I take you there?"

"Yes, Papa, when will we go?" he asked excitedly.

Papa told Daniel that they could start to collect what they needed in the morning, and then lifted the young boy in his arms and hugged him tightly, saying, "It's past your bedtime, so off to bed and tomorrow we will start a new adventure."

As Daniel marched up the stairs to his bedroom, he shouted down to Papa, "But how will we get there?"

Responding to the boy, Papa replied, "An air ship."

Daniel tossed and turned, struggling to sleep as his vivid imagination played wonderful tricks with his mind, he wondered how they would get to the Arctic Circle and what they would find there. Eventually exhausted, he fell sound asleep, dreaming of the next strange trip.

The next morning, after breakfast, the two inseparable companions went out into the backyard hunting for what they would need to get themselves to the Arctic Circle. Papa explained that they would need a basket that was big enough for both him and Daniel to get into.

Daniel suddenly chirped up, "What about Grandma's laundry basket?"

"A great idea!" exclaimed Papa. "But I don't think Grandma will be very pleased."

"Yeah, but we can put it back once we return from our adventure."

"OK," agreed Papa, thinking that's the main item sorted,

but wondering what on earth to do with all of Grandma's laundry in the meantime.

"What else will we need?" asked the inquisitive Daniel.

Papa explained to the lad that some rope and plastic tubing, both of which Papa had in his tool chest, would be needed. They would also require a linen sheet and at least fifty balloons. "But we will also need an empty pop bottle," said Papa.

"Well, that's easy," said Daniel and he took himself straight off to the fridge and took out a bottle of pop that had about a cupful of pop left in the bottle. Daniel poured the pop into his favourite Newcastle United cup and said to Papa, "There you go, one pop bottle!"

"Brilliant!" said Papa.

"I'm still not sure how we are going to get to the Arctic, Papa," asked the curious Daniel.

"All will be revealed, my trusted friend," Papa said, leaving the boy with more questions than answers.

Papa then took Daniel into the kitchen and opened one of the large draws that kept Grandma's cooking ingredients safe. Papa took from the draw a tub of baking soda and a bottle of white wine vinegar.

"Why do we need that, Papa?" asked the ever-questioning Daniel.

"All will be revealed in good time." As their list was almost complete, Papa and Daniel wandered up into town to get the one thing they did not have at home, the balloons.

Daniel walked alongside Papa, keen to ask a question but embarrassed to release the words from his mouth. Papa, knowing the boy so well, asked, "So what's on your mind?"

Shuffling in his shoes, Daniel mustered up his courage and asked, "Do you think we can take some chocolate on the trip, Papa, and *I REALLY* promise this time, I will share it with you."

This made Papa laugh and he smiled at his travel companion and said, "Of course you can take some chocolate, but maybe we'll take an extra bar just in case!"

"Thanks, Papa," echoed the boy's grateful reply.

Back at home, the two boys took their bits and pieces into the backyard and assembled it all ready for construction.

"Now, Daniel, I would like you to place six large stones in the bottom of the basket."

"Why, Papa?" asked a bemused boy.

"That will be our ballast."

Still none the wiser, Daniel smiled as if he knew exactly what ballast meant and carried on with his allocated task. The rope was tied to the basket in six equally spaced areas along the edge.

"Now that's all we can do for today," said Papa.

Tomorrow would be a long day and so Papa suggested that they should head indoors and recharge their batteries to be ready for the forthcoming weird adventure.

The following day, after pancakes and huckleberry jam, Papa's favourite, Daniel and Papa headed outside, ready to build the air ship that would transport them to the Arctic.

"Now, Daniel, you need warm clothes for this journey as the Arctic gets very cold. Grandma has made a flask of hot soup and some huckleberry jam sandwiches for later."

Whilst Daniel went to get into his warm clothes, Papa placed just the right amount of baking soda into the empty pop bottle then filled it to half way with the white wine vinegar; as he did so, the magical concoction started to froth, bubble and fizz. Papa placed the first balloon over the neck of the pop bottle and as if by magic the balloon began to inflate slowly. Out came Daniel, wrapped up perfectly.

Papa tied a knot in the balloon, then said, "Can you place this balloon under the sheet please, Daniel?"

Papa had already strategically placed the striped sheet over the ropes, well, thick string really.

Papa continued to inflate balloon after balloon until at least twenty were covered by the sheet, which they luckily found in Grandma's laundry basket. Then, all of a sudden, the sheet started to rise.

"Oh, Papa, what's happening?"

Papa explained that once all the balloons had been inflated, the air ship would be ready for lift off. "At the moment," Papa began to explain, "the six stones are holding down our air ship, that's called ballast."

"I knew that, Papa."

Papa chuckled at the boy's sense of humour.

The last of the forty balloons were filled and released to the sheet which itself had formed into a giant balloon shape. The other ten balloons would be needed for the return journey.

Papa said, "OK, Daniel, empty the six stones from the basket." Daniel removed the first stone, then the second and third and he felt the air ship rock gently back and forth. "In you get!" called Papa. The fourth and fifth stones were thrown from the basket and the ship was rising slowly, Daniel threw the last stone from the ship and the two drifted calmly into the sky before being carried off on a gentle breeze and in a northerly direction.

It was as if you could touch the clouds with your fingertips as bird after bird flew gracefully past the airborne ship. Far, far below people were now just specks on the land as the two enjoyed the peace and solitude this unique experience gave them. As they floated on the breeze that carried them northwards, Daniel smiled almost continuously, so mesmerized by this new experience.

"Wow, Papa, just wow!"

They drifted calmly through the sky until in no time at all, the Arctic Circle was in sight. Papa reached up to remove one balloon, then another and another until he had lessened the total by ten, the air ship drifted downward towards an amazing blanket of whiteness.

Excitedly, Daniel shouted "Papa, look, a polar bear!" Sure enough a giant bear as white as Grandma's sheets back home, strolled across the frozen surface looking up from time to time, perhaps wondering what this strange object was that was getting closer and closer. The bear appeared to shake his head in disbelief before wandering off.

The air ship closed in on the surface, touching down just before lunch and with such perfect ease, an aircraft pilot would have been proud of the landing.

"Six large pieces of ice please, Daniel," called Papa.

Daniel jumped like an athlete from the air ship and duly placed the ice into the bottom of the basket to act as their ballast.

As Papa clambered out of the basket, he put one foot on the ice and swung his other leg over the top of the basket; unfortunately, Papa didn't realise how slippery the ice was and fell onto his bottom, sliding and sliding down the ice away from the airship and definitely to the amusement of Daniel who laughed uncontrollably. Papa slid and slid and slid until he came to an abrupt stop! His short journey brought to an unceremonious halt by the big fat tummy of a walrus.

Unconcerned by the collision, the walrus turned to Papa and said, "I'm Wilson Walrus, pleased to meet you."

Papa was taken aback, but politely replied, "I'm Papa, equally pleased to meet you, Mr. Walrus, and over there is my grandson, Daniel."

Without any further explanation, the walrus smiled, turned and waddled away from the two boys, shouting, "Hope we meet again. By the way, make sure you have enough ballast to hold down your basket, it gets very windy here!"

Daniel was amazed at the spectacle of a talking walrus. He turned to Papa and said, "Wow, Papa, just wow!"

Rubbing his sore bottom, Papa made a suggestion. "I think now we can enjoy some chocolate?"

Papa knew that tell-tale sign; Daniel demonstrated that embarrassed and guilty look.

"Err, em, well, you know when we saw that polar bear, Papa?"

"Yes," he replied.

"Well, I ate the chocolate then. Sorry, Papa."

Secretly, Papa knew that the chocolate had been eaten and he really didn't mind, but he did enjoy playing games with his best friend.

Papa smiled at the young boy and said, "Just as well, we have soup and sandwiches and, of course, that extra bar of chocolate that we will keep for our return journey."

Stopping for a ten-minute break, Daniel and Papa felt warmed and fortified following the soup and huckleberry jam sandwiches made so lovingly by Grandma. Papa stood up, gathered a large handful of soft snow to make the perfect snowball and threw it at Daniel, missing by a long way. He laughed and turned to walk away but as he did, *THUMP!* An equally perfect snowball hit him in the back of the head; it turned out that Daniel was much better at snowball throwing than Papa.

"Come on, you win," Papa called out and off they went.

Trekking across the Arctic, Daniel produced his camera ready to take a picture of a beautiful arctic fox that was standing only a few meters away, totally unperturbed by the two visitors.

"Hello, I'm Ferdinand Fox, and you are?" the fox asked.
"I'm Daniel and this is Papa."
The fox asked the boys what they were doing, to which Daniel replied, "We are on an adventure; last week we went to see some grey-blue humpback whales and the week before that, we went to the Moon."
The fox laughed loudly, turned to look at Papa and said, "That boy has some imagination."
"Yes," replied Papa. "Although what he says is true."
Ferdinand fox laughed even louder to declare, "You as well." Without further chat, the fox turned full circle and headed across the ice, still laughing as he wandered off.
Just as the fox disappeared from sight and as if from nowhere, there appeared a massive reindeer with two calves by her side. Daniel was overcome with joy and waved frantically at the animal. The reindeer turned its head towards Daniel, nodded and wandered over.
"Hello, young boy, I'm Ruby Reindeer, and these are my two boys, Rascal and Robert."
"I am delighted to meet you; my name is Daniel and this is Papa."
"We saw your impressive air ship coming down to land," said Ruby. "Are you on an adventure?"
Daniel told the reindeer of his previous adventures and how the fox just laughed when they told him.
"Ha ha," said Ruby. "Don't take any notice of Ferdinand, he's quite mad."
Ruby and her two offspring turned and wandered off into the Arctic snow that had started to fall.
"It was nice meeting you three," Daniel called.
After another snowball fight, that Daniel won again, they made their way back to the air ship passing close to the

edge of the ice platform where they were greeted by a family of seals frolicking in the ice-cold water.

"Hi, guys, I'm Sally Seal and these are my friends. Be careful on the ice, won't you?"

"I'm Daniel and this is Papa," Daniel replied. "Thanks for the advice, we'll be very careful."

The seals barked together in harmony and then before Papa and Daniel knew it, they dove under the ice-cold water and were gone.

Daniel turned to Papa and said, "Wow, Papa, just wow!"

Just as they reached the air ship, a magnificent snowy owl flew across their path, Daniel quickly shouted, *"Too wit too woo!"*

Hearing this, the owl made an about-turn and flew back towards the boys, landing with grace on the side of the air ship basket.

"Howdy, guys," said the owl. "My name is Olivia."

Papa introduced himself and his grandson to the wonderful bird.

"What brings you to this place then, Daniel?" the beautiful owl asked.

"It's an adventure, Olivia," Daniel explained. "We have one most weekends."

Papa laughed and told Olivia Owl, "That's correct, although it's sadly now time to close this adventure and head home again."

"Well," Olivia said, "safe journey," and off she flew calling *"Too wit too woo"* as she glided with ease.

Daniel laughed at this and called out to the bird, *"Too wit too woo* right back at you, Olivia Owl!"

Papa explained to Daniel that snowy owls in the Arctic are active during the day unlike other owls that tend to come out at night.

"Wow, how do you know so much about animals and birds, Papa?" asked Daniel.

"The time I spent in the jungle, I taught Tarzan how to get from one tree to another," Papa laughed.

"Take me to the jungle, Papa, please."

"Well, perhaps one day."

The two boys climbed aboard the air ship and Papa quickly set about opening the pop bottle that still had the magic mixture in it; he produced the ten spare balloons and one by one he inflated these and Daniel placed them into the sheet. Wilson Walrus was right, it was getting windy and the ice blocks had already started to melt. The more the ice melted and the wind got stronger, the basket started to slide across the ice.

"Papa!" shouted a concerned Daniel. "What do we do?"

Just then, the largest polar bear anyone had ever seen wandered over to where the boys were now really struggling to hold on to the basket.

"Need some help?" the polar bear asked.

"Yes, please!" shouted Papa.

"Calm down then, I'm Preston and I'm in charge around here."

Preston Polar Bear grabbed four large pieces of ice and placed them gently into the basket and straight away the basket was once again under control.

"Phew!" said Papa turning to Preston, saying, "I'm Papa and this is Daniel, are we pleased that you came along."

The bear smiled and said, "I saw you coming in to land and I knew that it was going to get windy so I thought I'll stick around in case you needed help."

"Well," added Daniel, "we are very pleased you did, Preston."

"My pleasure," replied the bear. "But I must be off now; I need to make sure everything in the Arctic Circle is as it should be. Have a safe journey home."

The bear wandered off, disappearing into the snow within minutes.

With only one balloon left to inflate, Daniel began to remove the ice blocks from the bottom of the basket that were already starting to melt, making them easier to throw out of the basket. Soon the ship was lifting higher and higher into the dusky Arctic sky. Down below, they spotted Preston polar bear chatting with Wilson Walrus, he looked up and nodded his head as if to acknowledge a unique friendship, waved and then continued to chat.

The boys seemed to be making good progress until Daniel looked at Papa and realised there was a problem. Daniel knew his Papa so well; he just knew that look.

"What's the matter, Papa?" he asked.

"Well, we seem to be drifting to the West, when we need to go South; it appears the direction of the wind has changed."

A worried Daniel suggested, "Grandma won't be happy, Papa; you'll be in more trouble." Just then, as if by magic, a group of twenty albatrosses flew alongside the air ship.

One of the birds landed on the basket and said to Papa, "I'm Anton Albatross; you seem to be in a spot of bother, old chap?"

"Yes," replied Papa, "I'm Papa and this is my grandson,

Daniel. The wind has changed direction and we are heading away from home."

Anton explained that Preston had asked him and his group to keep a close watch on them as they headed away from the Arctic Circle.

"Right," said Anton. "My group will fly alongside you, and the wind from our massive wings will be enough to get you back in the direction for home."

What a spectacular sight; twenty of the largest sea birds flying alongside the air ship and sure enough, the craft slowly but surely started to change direction. The group of Albatrosses turned and without another word flew off into the evening sunset, the two boys waved and waved until the birds could no longer be seen.

The air ship drifted smoothly back towards Papa's house as if it now knew the way. In what felt like no time at all, Daniel and Papa could see the backyard from the air ship. Daniel waved frantically at Grandma who was stood in the yard waiting for them to return. They landed perfectly just before tea time and exactly as Papa had planned.

"First things first, Daniel," declared Papa. "Untie the ropes and release the balloons."

Daniel did exactly that and the balloons floated into the sky, leaving the basket to be returned to Grandma for her laundry and the sheet to go back on the washing pile.

"You boys must be very tired!" exclaimed Grandma.

"Not me," declared Daniel. He was just so keen to relay

the detail of his weird adventure to Grandma, telling all he had seen and done at the Arctic Circle.

"Well, I've had a very easy day," said Grandma, "I was going to do some washing but I couldn't find my laundry basket and the sheet that was in there has disappeared too, I don't suppose you two know anything about that?" said Grandma suspiciously.

The two boys looked at each other and with his sweetest smile, Daniel said, "No, Grandma, you know we've been out all day."

Chapter Four

The following week, Daniel visited Grandma and Papa earlier than usual to spend four days; his first words to Papa after walking through the door were "What is the adventure this week, Papa?"

"Well, nice to see you, Daniel," remarked Papa.

"Sorry, Papa," Daniel gave Papa a massive hug before repeating his earlier question.

"Something a little different," replied Papa.

After they had finished their pop and crisps, Papa said to young Daniel, "Did I ever tell you about the time I played professional football?"

Daniel smiled, asking for the details but confused as to how this could be any kind of adventure for him. He would soon find out.

"We need to go into the attic," Papa explained.

"Why?" Daniel asked.

"All will be revealed," replied Papa.

The boys climbed up the ladder leading them into the attic and were greeted by box after box scattered in a totally disorderly fashion.

"Now, Daniel," said Papa, "we are looking for a box with the word 'Magpies' written on it."

In the corner of the attic were at least six fishing rods, next to which there was an old chair, clearly used by previous grandchildren. There were boxes of games, fancy dress outfits neatly folded, ready for the next party. Two suitcases sitting ready for the next holiday and behind them lay the Christmas decorations waiting for the coming festive season.

Exhausted after moving so many boxes, Papa declared, "One day I must organise everything up here," to which Daniel very quickly retorted,

"You know that'll never happen, anyway, I'm sure Grandma knows where everything is and you would be in more trouble if you started to rearrange things."

Papa laughed and said, "Perhaps you're right, son, perhaps you're right."

Papa and Daniel moved box after box, but still couldn't find what they were looking for. Papa stood scratching his head until something caught the corner of his eye and he moved forwards to a set of four boxes so far untouched.

"Here it is!" declared Papa in a triumphant voice.

Blowing the dust from the box, he and the child sat down to open the package.

"This is a box of magic, a box of inspiration, a box filled with hope," Papa told Daniel.

The boy sat there amazed and curious as never before, desperate to see what was contained in the box. Papa gently removed the packaging from inside the box and smiled a childlike smile as he proudly pulled from the box a pair of old tattered football boots. He held them up high, expecting more of a response from Daniel other than a deflated look.

"Is that it, Papa?" asked the unimpressed young boy.

"These boots," Papa continued, "are not just ANY boots;

these were the boots of John Walker Richardson, born in 1864, perhaps the greatest ever English footballer."

"But, Papa, what's so special about these boots?"

"Well, you see, John Walker Richardson was my great grandfather and he passed the boots onto his son who then passed them onto his son, my father, and he gave them to me."

Daniel looked puzzled before asking, "Why did you not give the boots to my dad?"

Papa smiled and then said, "I trained your dad to be a secret agent instead. So now, it's your turn to receive them."

Not wanting to appear ungrateful, Daniel said, "OK, Papa," but it was obvious by the look on his face that he was far from impressed.

Papa continued to explain, "Family legend has it that these boots were given to John Walker Richardson in 1884 by a Native American Indian Chief called 'Clouds of Wisdom' and they possess a very special magic; my great grandfather went on to become not just an all-time great English footballer but the best Newcastle United right winger ever seen."

Papa knew that Daniel was an avid football supporter and, like Papa, loved the mighty magpies, Newcastle United.

"Try them on for size," Papa gestured to Daniel.

He took one of the boots and wondered what to make of it all but, nonetheless, he pulled the footwear over his toes and it was as if the boot slid onto his foot without any help. Puzzled by this, Daniel looked down and was amazed that the boot was firmly and comfortably encasing his right foot, by some miracle the laces were tied to perfection and it all happened without Daniel's assistance. He took the left boot and just slipped his foot in and incredibly the same thing happened. The boots in unison gripped the boy's feet, sending a tingling sensation into his toes. His feet felt light and unusual. He stood up, and the boots were the perfect fit as suddenly his feet started to dance, tapping on the floor of the attic. "What's happening, Papa?" the boy asked with some concern.

"The boots want to play football!" said Papa.

"Now we know they fit," said Papa, "you must take them off and promise one thing, only to wear the boots on match days and NEVER clean them."

Daniel looked at Papa, acknowledged his command but took it all with a pinch of salt. They climbed out of the attic and went downstairs where Grandma was waiting with lunch ready on the table.

"Ah, so you found those old boots," she said. "Has Papa told you the history of the boots?"

"Yes, Grandma," but he was still not terribly impressed. Unknown to him, more was to come!

Daniel was aware that he and Papa were going to the match on Sunday to watch their beloved Newcastle United take on their bitter rivals Sunderland in the cup. This was the biggest match of the season as the winners would be playing in the final at Wembley.

"So, you know we are going to the match on Sunday?"

"Yes, Papa,"

"Well, I've spoken with the manager Baffa and you are playing in the right-wing position."

"No!" laughed Daniel, his face turning red.

"Yes, you are!"

Papa was good friends with Baffa and often helped him out. He had already told the Newcastle manager of Daniel's skills.

Daniel would regularly practice his football skills with Papa in the local park, dribbling, shooting and generally learning how to control the ball. So they decided this was a good time to get some practice in.

On the way down to the park, Daniel looked at his Papa and quietly asked, "Do you think we could get some chocolate to share at halftime?"

"I'm sure we can do that," Papa agreed, smiling to himself and thinking, *I'll be lucky to get any!*

They headed home ready for some food; after they had eaten, they sat with Grandma talking of the days when Papa was a top footballer; the goals he had scored and the trophies he had won. After an hour and tired from his football practice, but also through eager anticipation of the game the next day, Daniel headed off to bed.

No matter how hard he tried, he could not sleep. He tossed this way and shuffled that way, his mind filled with a vision of himself in a black-and-white shirt playing against their arch enemy, Sunderland.

His mind raced with excitement until eventually exhausted by his own thoughts, he nodded off to sleep with a smile etched across his face.

The next morning, Grandma and Papa were already downstairs when Daniel came to the breakfast table. "Before any game, I always had pancakes and huckleberry jam," Papa said. Just then, Grandma placed a plate of her finest pancakes onto the table and Daniel took two and smothered them with Huckleberry jam. Daniel hardly said a word that morning; such was his excitement at playing for Newcastle United.

He demolished six golden pancakes, wiped the jam from his mouth, rubbed his tummy, then declared, "I'm off for a shower."

Daniel appeared from his room, hair still wet and his kit bag over his shoulder. He grabbed the box which contained the ancient boots and placed them into his bag. He stood there gazing at Papa, clearly very emotional. Papa put an arm around him and ushered him to the car.

Arriving at the home of Newcastle United, St James Park, Papa took Daniel through the players' entrance and down to the changing rooms where the players sat waiting for the pre-match talk from Baffa.

"Hello, Daniel," the players called out, knowing that today he would be their right winger. The shy young lad smiled at the footballers, all of his heroes packed into one room.

There was lots of laughter and jokes until the door swung open and in walked Baffa; the place was now silent as a mark of respect to the manager.

"I see you have all met Daniel," Baffa said. "He'll be on the right wing today."

"Yes, boss!" was the united response.

"We know what we have to do, so let's get out there and win this game," demanded Baffa.

Daniel unpacked his bag and gently placed his old boots on the floor; the other players looked but said nothing. Meanwhile, Daniel took the black and white shirt that was hanging next to him, pulled it over his shoulders, pulled on the black shorts, followed by the socks and then the boots. The boots instinctively gripped his feet and his toes just curled and tingled, something was happening to his feet, but what?

Out of the changing room the team marched and stood in the players' tunnel waiting for the opposition. Standing proud in his black and white shirt, he watched as the team's bitter rivals quickly stood side by side the Newcastle players. As Daniel stood there nervously, one of the Sunderland players noticed Daniel's boots and burst into hysterical laughter pointing at the very old and worn-out footwear; "Look at them boots," he scorned. Daniel was embarrassed like never before, his big day; his big chance to shine, his opportunity to mesmerize the crowd was ruined before it had even started.

Daniel felt dejected, beaten before he had even kicked the ball and ready to turn full-circle and head back to the changing room. Just then, he caught glimpse of Papa standing next to Baffa. A solitary tear rolled down Daniel's cheek as Papa marched along the line towards the boy at the same time offering a menacing look to the Sunderland player who had ridiculed his grandson. "Head up, son," Papa enthused, always able to get the boy to see sense. "Just remember what we spoke about and let your feet do the talking on the pitch, and I promise you, at the end of the game, you'll be the one laughing and they will be in tears."

Daniel never ever doubted Papa, they had done so much together, he was Daniel's rock and if he said it would all work out, then Daniel knew it would.

The proud young boy turned to the Sunderland player and smiled, refusing to be goaded by those in red and white shirts. Then the referee led the teams out of the tunnel and onto the pitch.

Wow, just wow! thought Daniel as the sold-out crowd erupted into thunderous applause. *What a feeling, what an atmosphere; this beats a trip to the Moon, outdoes an encounter with the grey-blue humpback whales and it's even better than a visit to the Arctic Circle.*

The teams were ready to do battle as the referee blew the whistle for kick-off. Sunderland immediately took possession of the ball and pushed it forwards to threaten the Newcastle goal, taking a shot that was easily saved by the Newcastle goalkeeper. The goalkeeper, seeing Daniel out wide, passed the ball straight to his feet, but before Daniel could control the ball, a Sunderland player charged at him, taking the ball and bundling the boy over onto the grass. Daniel stood up and wondered what was happening, he looked over to Papa who was on the touchline and shrugged his shoulders as if to say 'what do I do?' Papa simply smiled.

The ball had gone off the pitch and out of play so Papa beckoned Daniel over to the touchline and simply said to the boy, "Listen to the boots, relax, feel the boots on your feet, let the boots help you, let the boots play the game."

Away he ran and as the game re-started, Newcastle had the ball, a long pass fell to Daniel, but this time he relaxed his feet and felt the tingle in his toes as the boots worked their magic. Daniel scooped the ball up with his right foot, juggled it back and forth and set off at a blistering pace along the touchline. It was if the ball was stuck to his feet as he skipped past one player after another; but then from the corner of his eye he saw the unmistakable sight of Broody Dump, Sunderland's biggest and fiercest defender charging like a raging bull towards him. Daniel touched the ball from left to right, but still the defender closed in and with a look of determined menace etched on his face, he lunged at Daniel. Without the need to think; Daniel felt the boots thinking for him; he flicked the ball into the air, onto his chest, raised both feet from the ground and the Sunderland defender went flying past, missing both Daniel and the ball, much to the amusement of the crowd as the fans erupted into the chant "DANIEL, DANIEL, DANIEL!"

Encouraged by this, he danced his way forward, quickly noticing his teammate Calum Spearer running into the penalty area; he instantly floated the ball over the heads of the other Sunderland players and onto the head of

Calum who rose up and headed the ball into the back of the net. The crowd went wild, clapping and cheering their heroes. Daniel smiled and knew instantly what Papa meant about the boots; they were indeed magic. He thought to himself, *Wow, just wow!*

The game kicked off again. The Sunderland players struggled to get hold of the ball as the Newcastle players at every opportunity gave the ball to Daniel and he and his nimble feet danced time after time along the touchline, delivering perfect cross time after time for his team. At halftime, it was Newcastle 4 Sunderland 0.

Wow, just wow, thought Daniel as he headed in for the halftime break, waving to the adoring crowd as he left the field.

Baffa congratulated the team, not selecting any one player individually, simply stating, "More of the same to wrap this game up, lads." Out they went for the second half and immediately Sunderland went on the attack. The ball zipped from one side of the pitch to the other but however hard they tried, they couldn't get the ball into a position that allowed them to score a goal.

The ball was cleared and soon landed at the feet of Daniel, he curled his toes in the boots and away he went, dribbling past one player then another and another, Daniel showed all of his magic. Suddenly, he realised Broody Dump was once again bearing down on him with the look of a man determined to get his revenge, his fiery eyes focussed on Daniel. When he was only inches away, Daniel used all his skill to gently place the ball between Broody's legs, swerving around him like a tornado and leaving him far behind. Again the crowd was enthralled by the boy's trickery. As Daniel reached the goal, the goalkeeper ran towards him to block the awaited move but Daniel lobbed the ball over his head and straight into the back of the net! The crowd stood up and went wild and as he calmly turned to salute his fans, his teammates surrounded him, smothering him with congratulations.

Newcastle went on to dominate the game and finished by winning 8 goals to nil. Daniel was the star of the game and at the final whistle; his teammates lifted him onto their shoulders for a celebratory run around the pitch. It was a resounding victory, enjoyed by the crowd, the team, Papa and most of all, Daniel.

"You see, dreams do come true," said Papa as he was the first to congratulate Daniel as he left the pitch.

"All I can say is, wow, Papa, just wow!"

They headed to the changing room. As he went into the room full of his heroes, one by one they congratulated young Daniel who was overcome with happiness and emotion. Before leaving, Daniel and Papa thanked all the players and, of course, the manager Baffa.

As Papa and Daniel drove out of the city back home to where Grandma would be waiting, the two relived every minute of the game, especially the moment young Daniel scored a superb goal at the home of football.

"Oh and Papa, guess what I have in my pocket?"
Papa was curious to know what the lad had and replied,
"Do tell."
"Chocolate!" declared Daniel. "And this time, I didn't eat
it all so we CAN share it."
Papa shook his head and laughed.
Back at home Papa reminded Daniel of two things; only
wear the boots on a match day and NEVER ever clean
them.
"You have my word," said Daniel. And he never did...

Coming soon
Blenkinsop Blabbermouth and the Fearsome Pirate

(Further Adventures of Daniel and Papa)